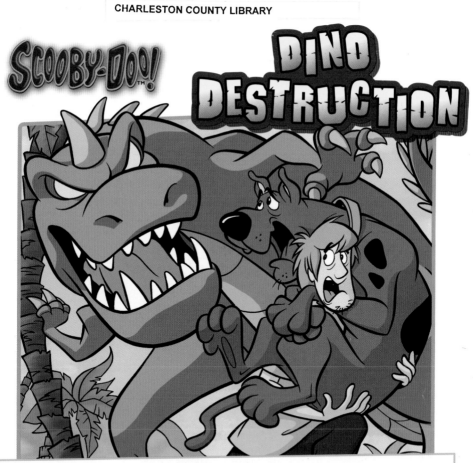

Adapted by Lee Howard
Interior illustrated by Alcadia Snc
Cover illustrated by Duendes del Sur
Based the episode "3-D Destruction" by Ed Scharlach

WWW.ABDOPUBLISHING.COM

Reinforced library bound edition published in 2015 by Spotlight, a division of ABDO
PO Box 398166, Minneapolis, Minnesota 55439.
Spotlight produces high-quality reinforced library bound editions for schools and libraries.
Published by agreement with Warner Bros. Entertainment Inc.

Printed in the United States of America, North Mankato, Minnesota.
052014   072014

 THIS BOOK CONTAINS
RECYCLED MATERIALS

LIBRARY OF CONGRESS CATALOGING-IN-PUBLICATION DATA

Howard, Lee.
 Scooby-doo comic storybook / adapted by Lee Howard ; art by Alcadia Snc. -- Reinforced library bound ed.
  pages cm
 Four graphic novels, previously published separately.
 ISBN 978-1-61479-281-9 (#1: A haunted Halloween) -- ISBN 978-1-61479-282-6 (#2: A merry scary holiday) -- ISBN 978-1-61479-283-3 (#3:
Camp Fear) -- ISBN 978-1-61479-284-0 (#4: Dino destruction)
 1. Graphic novels. I. Howard, Lee. Haunted Halloween. II. Howard, Lee. Merry scary holiday. III. Howard, Lee. Camp fear. IV. Howard, Lee. Dino
destruction. V. Alcadia (Firm) VI. Scooby-Doo (Television program) VII. Title.
 PZ7.7.H74Sco 2015
 741.5'973--dc23
                    2014005381

Spotlight
A Division of ABDO
www.abdopublishing.com

Scooby-Doo and the kids from Mystery, Inc. are on vacation in Costa Rica. They decide to check out the local natural history museum.

THIS MUSEUM IS FAMOUS FOR ITS WORK ON DINOSAUR FOSSILS AND BONES.

I'M THE MUSEUM CURATOR, DR. GUTIERREZ. I HOPE YOU ENJOY OUR DINOSAUR EXHIBIT.

Next, the gang meets Melbourne O'Reilly, a legendary fossil hunter.

G'DAY, MATES.

WOW, IT'S AN HONOR TO MEET YOU! I JUST SAW YOUR PICTURE ON A MAGAZINE COVER. YOU WERE HAND-CATCHING PIRANHAS IN THE AMAZON RIVER!

AH, THAT WAS A DAY AT THE BEACH COMPARED TO FINDING THESE DINO BONES. I WAS LUCKY TO GET OUT OF THE JUNGLE ALIVE!
WHAT DO YOU MEAN?
SOME FOLKS SAY THERE'S A CURSE ON THESE BONES. WHOEVER REMOVES THEM FROM THEIR RESTING PLACE WILL SUFFER THE DINOSAUR SPIRIT'S REVENGE!

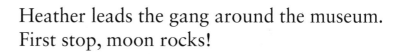
Heather leads the gang around the museum. First stop, moon rocks!

WE'RE ONE OF THE FEW MUSEUMS TO EXHIBIT REAL MOON ROCKS. THAT'S THE EXCAVATOR THE ASTRONAUTS USED TO RECOVER THEM.

Next, she takes the gang on a tour of the old mineshaft. Then it's back to the auditorium for a special presentation.

Dr. Gutierrez introduces a new documentary about dinosaurs.

WE'RE SO PLEASED TO HAVE THE DIRECTOR, J.J. HOKOMOTO, HERE WITH US TODAY.

IT'S HUGE! IT'S SCARY! IT'S RIGHT IN YOUR LAP! IT'S THE GIGANTOSAURUS IN 3-D!

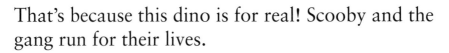

That's because this dino is for real! Scooby and the gang run for their lives.

Fortunately, everyone manages to escape unharmed. But the museum's exhibits aren't so lucky. . . .

That's when a stranger approaches Dr. Gutierrez.
I'M LUIS SEPEDA, AND I REPRESENT THE PEOPLE OF THE CENTRAL VALLEY. YOU HAVE STOLEN OUR SACRED BONES FROM THEIR RESTING PLACE. PLEASE, I BEG YOU TO RETURN THEM.
I HAVEN'T STOLEN ANYTHING. THE BONES WILL REMAIN HERE IN THE MUSEUM.
IF YOU DON'T RETURN THOSE BONES, A *GREAT DISASTER* WILL BEFALL YOU!

Melbourne O'Reilly brings the gang back to the mine to look for the dinosaur.

THE FOOTPRINTS LEAD THIS WAY.

Shaggy steps into a puddle of goop.

I THINK IT'S DINOSAUR DROOL, SHAGGY.

LIKE, WHAT?!

The next thing Shaggy finds is a lot less disgusting . . . gold!

The mine's tunnels branch off in three different directions.

WHICH WAY SHOULD WE GO?

LET'S SPLIT UP AND LOOK FOR CLUES.

I'LL TAKE THE FIRST TUNNEL.

Fred, Velma, and Daphne take the second tunnel.
That leaves Scooby and Shaggy with the third.

The two buddies haven't gone far when they hear a rumbling sound. . . .

Now the dinosaur's got the whole gang cornered!

It's Shaggy and Scooby to the rescue! Fred, Velma, and Daphne pile into the railroad cart.

The gang manages to outrun the dinosaur. They find an old exit that takes them to the jungle outside the museum.

AH! YOU MADE IT OUT SAFELY. I'M ALL RIGHT, TOO, MATES.

I'M PRETTY SURE THAT'S NOT A REAL DINOSAUR. BUT SOMEONE WANTS US TO BELIEVE IT IS. . . .

The kids head back inside to do a little more investigating.

ICK! YOU'RE TRACKING IN THAT DROOL WE FOUND EARLIER.

ISN'T THAT PROOF THERE'S A REAL DINOSAUR?

WAIT, I'VE SEEN THIS KIND OF STUFF BEFORE! IT'S USED TO MAKE COSMETICS.

The gang goes straight to Dr. Gutierrez's office.

I'M TESTING ONE OF THE DINOSAUR BONES TO SEE HOW OLD IT IS.

Velma runs some of the suspects' pictures through face-recognition software.

WHAT ABOUT MELBOURNE O'REILLY? SEEMS LIKE HE WOULD DO ANYTHING TO BE A HERO.

Next she runs a picture of Señor Sepeda.

I HAVE A FUNNY FEELING ABOUT THIS GUY AND HIS ANCIENT CURSES. . . .

JEEPERS! ACCORDING TO INTERPOL, HE'S A CON MAN! HE'S WANTED FOR SELLING ANCIENT RELICS ON THE BLACK MARKET.

The next thing Scooby and Shaggy know, they're waiting for the dinosaur to attack!

LIKE, WHY ARE WE ALWAYS THE ONES WHO END UP AS BAIT?

YOO-HOO!

GRRR!

The plan works! The dinosaur follows Shaggy and Scooby out of the mine and into the jungle.

Then it crashes through the glass entrance and chases them into the museum!

Shaggy and Scooby lead the dinosaur straight to the dinosaur bones exhibit—and into Fred's trap!

Fred pulls a rope, and a huge skeleton crashes down on the dinosaur.

But Fred has underestimated the dinosaur's strength. The enormous creature flexes its back and breaks loose!

The dinosaur has disappeared again! But Velma has an idea. . . .

I THINK I'VE FIGURED IT OUT! LET'S GET EVERYONE TO COME BACK TO THE AUDITORIUM.

Once the audience is in their seats, Velma begins her slideshow.

SHAGGY AND I WENT BACK TO THE MINE AND DID A LITTLE EXPERIMENT. USING A SUBWOOFER, WE PROVED THAT THE ONLY LIVING CREATURES INSIDE THE MINE ARE BATS.

NO OTHER PERSON OR ANIMAL COULD ENDURE THIS SOUND.

GRRRR!

THIS COLLEGE STUDENT IS A VERY TALENTED ART MAJOR—CAPABLE OF DESIGNING A DINOSAUR TO FIT OVER AN EXCAVATOR.

LIKE, SHE'S AN ART MAJOR AND A GOLD MINER. GET IT?

WHEN WE TESTED THE DINOSAUR BONES, WE DISCOVERED THEY ALL CAME FROM DIFFERENT PERIODS OF PREHISTORY—AND EVEN FROM DIFFERENT DINOSAURS!